CROWN OF BLOOD AND DUTY

House Of Blood And Roses

LAURA GREENWOOD

© 2024 Laura Greenwood

All rights reserved. This book or parts thereof may not be reproduced in any form, stored in any retrieval system, or transmitted in any form by any means – electronic, mechanical, photocopy, recording or otherwise – without prior written permission of the published, except as provided by United States of America copyright law. For permission requests, write to the publisher at "Attention: Permissions Coordinator," at the email address; lauragreenwood@authorlauragreenwood.co.uk.

Visit Laura Greenwood's website at:

www.authorlauragreenwood.co.uk

Cover by Vampari Designs

Crown Of Blood And Duty is a work of fiction. Names, characters, places, and incidents are the products of the author's imagination or are used fictitiously. Any resemblance to actual persons, living or dead, businesses, companies, events, or locales is entirely coincidental.

If you find an error, you can report it via my website. Please note that my books are written in British English: https://books.authorlauragreenwood.co.uk/errorreport

To keep up to date with new releases, sales, and other updates, you can join my mailing list via my website or The Paranormal Council Reader Group on Facebook.

Blurb

The duty of any princess is to do what she's told, but when Agnes is assigned a new bodyguard, all of that goes out of the window.

The last person Agnes ever expected to be employed as her sworn shield is the man she left behind when she was forced to become a vampire, but now he's not only in her life, but always there, reminding her of what they once shared. And what they can no longer have.

Hector never thought he'd see Agnes again, and now fate has brought them back together, he's not sure he's going to be able to let her go, even if he knows he should.

With the King determined to find a political match

for Agnes, time is ticking and the two of them have to decide what's more important to them - love or duty.

-

Crown Of Blood And Duty is a standalone connected to the House Of Blood And Roses series. It is a steamy vampire romantasy featuring a forbidden second chance m/f romance, vampires, and vampire royalty.

Chapter 1

I flip the page in my book but don't really pay attention to the words written there. I'm not entirely sure what's gotten into me, but I feel as if something bad is coming my way.

Maybe I just haven't drunk enough blood today. That can make anyone a bit jittery, and is thankfully something I can easily fix.

I set down my book and get to my feet, intending to go find one of the servants so I can ask them to fetch me some. There's every chance that isn't the problem, but it isn't exactly going to hurt for me to have some.

Before I can get to it, the door swings open and my lady's maid steps inside.

"Your Highness," she says with a curtsy. "His Majesty, the King, is here to see you."

I nod, trying my best to cover the brief panic within me. I have no idea what my father wants, but I can count on one hand the number of times he's come to my rooms in the four years I've lived in the palace. If he's here, then it's not for a social visit.

"Would you ask him if he wishes for refreshments, Maude?" Is that the right thing to do when the King visits? Despite *being* a princess, no one has given me any instruction on the way this part works.

"Of course, Your Highness," she responds without skipping a beat. Either she's expecting my instructions, or she's very good at pretending.

"I'd like a goblet of blood for myself. If the King doesn't wish for anything, I'll take it after he's gone."

Maude nods and curtsies again before disappearing to do as I've asked.

I look around my sitting room and try to decide where it's best to be when Father arrives, but can't decide. I wish all of this came easier to me, but it seems that I'm lacking somewhat in that department.

I straighten my skirts and try to make sure everything is in place. If I can't work out where to put myself in the room, the least I can do is try and make sure I look presentable, and like a proper princess.

Father sweeps into the room, wearing all black and cutting a striking figure while not looking a day over thirty. It's strange to think I look about the same age as my father, but that's just how vampire ageing works.

"Your Majesty," I say, dipping into a deep curtsy.

"Daughter," he responds in a cool collected tone, but I don't expect anything different from him. Despite the rumours saying that he loved my mother, I never saw much fatherly affection for him on his visits to the human town. And even less since I came here, though that could be due to the fact his queen hates me as a reminder of his affair. Most vampires just have their dhampir children with whatever human women crosses their path, they don't keep a mistress and have multiple children with her over the years. So while it's perfectly normal for me and my brother to have been brought to court and given full status as children of the king, I can understand why she doesn't want me around.

I push my thoughts aside and try to focus on the

situation at hand. "Did my maid ask if you wished for any refreshments?"

"She did, but I won't be here long enough for that. I came to speak with you."

I nod, but stay silent. With my father, it's always better to listen first, especially when there's no knowing what mood he's in.

"I'm assigning a sworn shield to you," he says.

I stare at him. "Why?" The question slips out before I can think better of it.

He sighs and gives me a look that I'm reasonably sure means he'd rather I didn't question him quite so bluntly. "Because there are rumblings amongst the nobility."

"Aren't there always?" I murmur.

"Agnes," he says firmly, reminding me of my place with little more than my name. "The rumblings are stronger than normal and seem to be birthing some plots. It seems as if there's a faction at court that wish to depose me, and they may use you to do it."

"With two brothers ahead of me in the succession, I doubt it."

Father sighs. "I should have had you educated at court."

If he had, I'd probably be dead already. The

Queen would have found it far easier to rid herself of an unwanted dhampir as opposed to the fully turned vampire I am now.

"They will marry you," Father says when I don't respond. "And in doing so, they can decide your brothers are in the way and have them killed, along with me."

"Oh." I grimace, hating the thought of anything happening to either of my brothers.

"So you are to keep your sworn guard with you at all times, no matter where you are. He goes with you to eat, he watches while you entertain guests, and he sleeps at your door. Do you understand?"

"Yes, Father," I respond through my desire to protest. "How long will the security measures be in place?"

"That depends on how long it takes to get the threat under control. And how long will it take for me to arrange a marriage that benefits House Soveguine for you."

I blink a couple of times. "You wish to marry me off?"

"You're a princess, Agnes. It is your job to further our family's goals by marrying well. And the next Golden Moon is barely a year away, it's time you found you your first husband."

"My first husband," I repeat.

"It is likely you will have more over the long span of your life," he says offhandedly. "Each time a marriage ends, you'll return to my care and I'll make the most advantageous match possible for you."

In other words, each time a husband of mine dies, he'll marry me off to the next highest bidder, on and on until he's gone and Marcus is on the throne. Then I'll just be the sister of a king instead of the daughter of one.

I force a smile, knowing there's no point arguing and that if I'm going to find a way out of this situation, then it means not drawing Father's attention. "Of course, Father." I dip into a curtsy.

"I'm glad you agree."

Hardly. But I've also come to realise that most vampires view their children as expendable, and I want to live too much to risk that.

Father clicks his fingers and a guard walks in. His armour shines in the torchlight, but it's his face that draws my attention.

My eyes widen and it's all I can do not to gasp as I recognise the curly brown hair and the dark green eyes that have featured in many of my dreams, both before I became a vampire and after.

Thoughts of what used to be drift through my mind. Of summer days by the river, and winters huddled next to the fire. Though they're not the most dangerous of the memories. Lips whispering against skin and fingers brushing against one another fill my mind.

I can almost taste his name on the tip of my tongue but I refrain from saying it.

His gaze meets mine and I can tell I'm not the only one in shock from the meeting. He didn't realise it would be me he was serving either. He gets down on one knee and dips his head. "Princess."

I clear my throat. "Rise, sir," I say, at a loss for what else to say. My voice cracks and I don't look at my father for fear he'll realise there's a past between me and the man who is now sworn to protect me.

"I am not a knight, Your Highness," he responds as he does as I commanded.

"Then what should I call you?" I ask, meeting his gaze and seeing all kinds of things there that I don't know what to do with.

"Hector."

"Very well, Hector."

He reacts visibly to me saying his name, no doubt thinking of all the other times I said it.

Back when we both thought we were human.

Father clears his throat. "I'll leave you to it. I expect you at the banquet tomorrow evening."

"Of course, Father," I respond with a curtsy.

Hector bows deeply as Father leaves. I follow him to the double doors and look around to make sure no one is around before slamming them shut.

I turn around and lean against them, staring at the man in front of me and barely believing my eyes. "You're supposed to follow me?" I ask.

"Yes, Princess."

"Please don't call me that." My voice cracks as I say the words and I take a step forward. "Not when we're alone, I can't bear it."

He wavers. "It's the proper way to address you."

"Not for you, it isn't."

He swallows hard. "Very well, Agnes."

My breath catches in my throat at the sound of my name on his lips once more. I never thought I'd hear it again, and now he's here, standing in my room.

"How are you here?" I ask.

"Much the same way you are, I suspect," Hector responds. "I was brought up to the castle on the Golden Moon, given blood, and woke up a vampire."

I wet my lips and his gaze instantly drops to

them, making me think of the dozens of kisses we shared before.

"I didn't know you were the princess when I was assigned the position," he says. "I didn't know you were here at all."

"I didn't find out until the night of the Golden Moon," I respond, my heart racing as I get to give the explanation I've thought about countless times before but never seriously thought I'd be able to give him. "Mama sat me and Lincoln down and told us that the man who visited us sometimes was our father and that he was a vampire. She still omitted the royalty part."

"I guess it made some of the lessons she was giving you make more sense."

Without meaning to, a small smile lifts at my lips. "It did. Now I know why she spent hours teaching me the proper manners of addressing various nobles. I never thought it would be useful."

"I remember you complaining about them. And the history lessons." He seems to have relaxed a little now the two of us are alone.

"So many history lessons. Lincoln loved them."

"I know. When we were ten, he used to follow you around reciting them all." He steps forward, then thinks better of it. "How is he?"

"He's Lincoln," I respond. Though that's not entirely true. He's been struggling with what he is more than I have, though I suspect that's partly because I've been lucky to be more sheltered since coming to the palace than he has.

Hector nods, looking like he wants to say so much more than that. I do too, but it's been four years, and I'm not entirely sure what to say either.

"I'm glad to see you," I whisper.

"Likewise, Agnes."

The door behind me opens before I can respond and I do my best to straighten my dress even though nothing about it has changed, it just feels as if an intimate moment has been interrupted.

"Your blood, Your Highness," Maude says, holding out a golden cup to me.

"Thank you," I say, taking it from her with a shaky hand. "This is my new sword shield," I say, gesturing to Hector.

She gives him what seems to be an approving look. A hint of jealousy rears up within me even though I know it's misplaced. It's been four years, Hector has probably moved on, and I wouldn't blame him considering that I just disappeared after the Golden Moon.

"Would you see that a bed is set up for him outside my chambers?" I ask the maid. "And that Hector has everything he desires? My father's orders are strict."

"Of course, Your Highness." She dips into a curtsy and disappears out of the room, leaving us alone once more.

Hector studies me intently. "You command people well."

"I always worry that if I don't act like a princess, someone will report it back to my father."

"And you're not worried I'll do the same?"

I meet his gaze, seeing our history written between us and I know my answer. "No."

Pride crosses his face and he makes no attempt to hide it.

If I have to have a guard following me around all the time, then at least it's him, someone I know, and someone I can trust.

Even if it's already hard to shake the memories of what we once were to one another.

Chapter 2

The banquet hall is full of chatter, but none of it is directed at me. If anything, the people in the room are talking *over* me and ignoring me completely.

I look across the table to where Lincoln is supposed to be sitting, but he's not there. Either Father didn't command him to come, or my brother has decided it's best to ignore the formal dinner. I don't really blame him, these events aren't exactly fun.

"You look positively bored, sister," Marcus says as he takes the empty seat beside me.

"That's because everyone seems to have forgotten I'm not just a pretty ornament," I respond to my half-brother, picking up my wine glass and swilling it around. "No one even considers that I might have opinions of my own, so assumes I'm not worthy of conversation."

"I'm sure you have many interesting insights you could offer the court," my half-brother says.

"Right now my insight is that your mother is looking at me as if she wants to kill me just because you're speaking to me," I point out, raising my glass to the queen.

She scowls and looks away.

I sigh. "She really doesn't like me, does she?"

"She doesn't know you," Marcus responds, reaching over to pick up a grape and popping it into his mouth. "To her, you're the symbol that our father loved another woman."

"He just did what every other man here is expected to do and found a human lover to create dhampirs for when there aren't enough true-born vampire children."

"Except me," Marcus mutters.

"Are you really trying to tell me you're sad about that?" I take a sip of my wine.

He sighs. "Not really. I don't have much interest in seducing anyone. But a cage is a cage no matter what it looks like."

I raise an eyebrow. "You're really going to talk to me of cages?"

"We're all in one, sister. My mother included. And here you are, a reminder that Father kept going to your mother. It isn't just you, but Lincoln too. Most men choose to only have one child with each human lover."

"Maybe it was just easier for him to return. I can't say I've thought to ask about it." And neither am I going to. It sounds like the kind of question I don't actually want an answer to.

"None of it matters, you're at court now, and there's nothing my dear mother can do about it but glare at you from across the table."

I snort. "I wouldn't count on that. I've been here long enough to know that court is ruthless. Wasn't it just last week that House Forbane lost their heir because of a feud with his brother?"

"That's different, that's a matter of him becoming an heir."

"And you think your mother killing me wouldn't be? I didn't take you for a fool, Marcus."

My brother chuckles. "I'm not a fool, I just understand how things work around here. Neither you or Lincoln are a threat to my position."

"Depends who father marries me off to," I mutter. "Any idea who he's considering?" I'm assuming Marcus will know, as the crown prince, he seems to be involved with decisions I'm not party to. Including who I'm going to marry.

"You're not going to like the answer."

I sit up in my chair. "So you *do* know."

"Yes, it's been the subject of the last couple of council meetings."

I stare at him. "Father only told me yesterday. Am I not supposed to have a say in this?"

Marcus grimaces, and I have my answer. I should count myself lucky that he's willing to tell me what's going on so I'm not taken completely by surprise.

"All right, just tell me who he's considering." It must be bad if Marcus is reluctant to tell me.

"House Forbane's new heir."

"Right, so at least one person who is capable of murder. That's great for me."

"They'll all be capable of murder, Agnes. This is court. The other options are Lord Drewforth…"

"He's older than Father," I protest.

"The younger brother of Lord Hexamble," Marcus continues as if I haven't protested.

"He's not too objectionable, I suppose." Though the thought of having to end up with someone just because my father wants it doesn't sit well within me.

"And Lord Falgrove."

I stare at him. "You can't be serious?"

Marcus nods.

"I've heard what he does to his wives, and he's still married. Please tell me there's at least another option. Preferably close to my age and doesn't have a reputation for beating his wives."

"The only other option that was talked about was the heir to House Rothorne. Mother is against it and says there's no need for it when our Houses are already united by her marriage to Father. But Father isn't convinced that the bond is as secure as it could be, and she can hardly argue about that."

"I didn't think House Rothorne had an heir currently?" I look over to where Lord Fallmartin is, almost as if I expect an heir to have appeared beside him.

"They don't, but Lord Fallmartin has assured us that he'll have one on the next Golden Moon."

"So my current best-case scenario is that if I wait a year, I'll marry some newly turned eighteen-year-old vampire, become your mother's niece-in-law, and potentially end up with someone who might be nice, but could also be worse than all of the rest of them put together?"

"More likely, Father will marry you off to one of

the others long before the year is out," Marcus responds. "But he sees it as just your first husband. Maybe you'll have better luck with your second?"

"Ha! And that's what I should hope for, is it? That my second husband is better than my first?"

Marcus grimaces. "Pretty much."

"I wish you were king," I mutter, flopping back into my seat.

"Don't say that," he hisses under his breath. "Have you any idea how much trouble you could get us both into if the wrong person heard that?"

"Doesn't stop it being true," I respond. "You wouldn't marry me off to someone just for the political clout."

"It's how things are done, Agnes."

"Oh, and where's *your* wife? Where's Lincoln's? Lord Fallmartin wants me to marry the heir to House Rothorne, well isn't one of his nieces unmarried? They could have you."

"They're my cousins," Marcus reminds me.

"All right, then why not Linc?" I look over to the empty chair where my other brother should be. He's not required to come to the banquets the same way as I am. He doesn't get paraded around to be shown off as something pretty and nothing else.

"Would you really want Lincoln to be married off like that?"

I sigh. "Of course not. I don't want any of us to be."

Marcus gives me a pitying look that makes me feel worse than anything else he could say.

"I'm not feeling well, I'm going to retire."

"You're a vampire, you can't get sick," he reminds me.

"Then you're going to have to make up an excuse for me." I rise to my feet and dust off my dress. "Good night, brother."

"I'm sorry if I upset you."

I reach out and put a hand on his shoulder. "You just told me the truth. And I love you for it. Enjoy the rest of the banquet."

His forced smile suggests that might not be possible. "Good night."

I nod and turn to make my exit. Hector moves away from the wall and falls into step behind me without saying a single word. I hate that we can't talk during these events, his presence would make things much more palatable.

It isn't until we're back in my rooms with the door firmly shut behind me that I let out a sigh of relief. "I'm glad that's over," I murmur.

"Who was that you were talking to?"

My lips quirk up into a smile. "Jealous?"

He chuckles uneasily. "I have nothing to be jealous of."

I turn around to face him, bringing the two of us a lot closer together than it's safe for us to be. "Nothing to be jealous of because you don't think anyone can live up to you? Or because you're over me?"

"That's not a question I should answer," he murmurs, his voice low and inviting.

My breathing hitches, his answer stirring something within me that I thought had been put away. "It was my brother," I respond. "Well, my half-brother. He was telling me unfortunate news."

"Is everything all right?"

"No." I step away. "Would you unlace me?"

He blinks a couple of times. "Unlace you?"

I nod. "I can't get out of my dress on my own, and I don't want to disturb Maude, the kitchens should be sending up some of the leftover food from the feast at any moment, and I don't want her to miss out."

"You have food brought here for your staff?"

"Of course. Please? Unlace me."

He nods stiffly and steps towards me. I turn my

back to him, only realising what a mistake this is when his fingers start to deftly untangle the laces on the back of my dress. I don't know if he does it on purpose, but it feels like he's going tantalisingly slowly.

The only thing I'm able to think of is the touch of his hand and the brush of his fingers through the thin fabric of my undergarments.

I'm caught in the moment, only able to focus on how close he is and nothing more.

"We should keep more distance between us," he murmurs, his breath brushing against my ear and sending a delightful shiver down my spine.

"No one knows," I respond, feeling his fingers get to the bottom of the laces holding my dress in place. The shoulder of my gown slips down, and I can feel the heat of his gaze on my bare skin, even if I know that's impossible.

"You don't know that."

"We're alone." I turn around, the movement causing more of my dress to slip off.

"This could all be some kind of test." The desire in his eyes is almost impossible to ignore.

I meet his gaze, trying to think clearly, but the only thing I'm aware of is the longing to be close to him again. To feel his hands against my skin and hear him say my name in the way only a lover would.

I hold up my dress, trying not to let it slip down more for fear that it'll cause more temptation between us than it should.

"I don't want to lose you again," I whisper, putting out the truth I know in my heart.

"Then we can't give into this," he says firmly. "We're putting ourselves in danger by even entertaining the notion." He finally steps away, putting much needed, and much hated, space between us.

I nod, aching deeper than I ever have before. I thought waking up the morning after the Golden Moon and realising I wasn't going to see him again was bad, but this is worse. He's going to be there all the time, close enough to touch but out of reach at the same time. We're going to be relegated to accidental touches and longing looks.

And at the end of it all, I'm going to be married to someone I don't even know, or have a choice in, and he's going to be further away than ever.

Fate has certainly been cruel to bring him back to me just to take him away once more.

Chapter 3

I straighten my mask and make sure everything is in place before I approach the double doors. The servants throw them open and allow me to enter the ballroom.

"Princess Agnes of House Soveguine," the herald calls.

I roll my eyes. What's the point of having a masked ball if they're just going to announce who I am as I enter?

Without giving any outward signal of my annoyance, I make my way down the steps, ignoring all of the people staring at me as I make the journey. I wish I didn't have to do this with so many eyes on me. But this is my lot in life. I'm a princess and it's my reality.

The guests part as I get to the bottom, and I try to work out who is who. It's mostly possible from the colours they're wearing, vampires aren't exactly known for being subtle when it comes to the pride in their Houses.

A man in a blue jacket and a matching mask steps forward, bowing deeply. "Might I have this dance, Princess?"

"Of course, Lord Falgrove," I respond through gritted teeth. I'd rather *not* dance with a man older than Father, or one who has a reputation of hurting his wives, but I also know that turning him down isn't an option either. Not with so many people watching.

He takes my hand in his, and I find myself grateful for my gloves so I don't have to touch his skin. Despite his handsome face and the fine figure he cuts in his expensive clothing, there's no escaping the revulsion I feel at being in his presence. This man is dangerous, and every part of me is screaming that I should get away from him.

He leads me onto the dance floor just as the music starts to play. I shoot a glance at the throne to see Father watching me with a pleased expression, seemingly happy with the direction this is taking. While the masquerade is just a ball, I wouldn't be surprised to learn he's having all of my potential suitors dance with me tonight.

Lord Falgrovebegins the waltz, his body uncomfortably close to mine. Even though he doesn't look it, I can't get his age out of my head, or the fact that this is one of the prospects Father is considering for my husband.

I look through the crowd, trying to find where Hector is. I was brought here by standard palace guards, but I have to believe he's here somewhere.

"If you have a chance to speak to the King about the proposal I gave him, will you tell him that I'm willing to gift him my castle at the edge of the kingdom," Lord Falgrove says.

"Your castle?" I echo.

"Yes. It might be far away, but in midsummer, there is barely any sun, it is truly the perfect summer retreat. I would gift it to him in exchange for a positive outcome to my proposal." He moves us with ease through the dance while he speaks, which is just as well, because otherwise, I might have lost my step.

"You're offering a bribe so he'll agree to let us marry?" I can't keep the surprise out of my voice. At least I'm not questioning him about his still-living wife.

"Being the consort of a royal princess is no small matter," he responds. "And my son would be king."

"My father still lives, and there are two brothers ahead of me in the succession," I remind him coolly. "Both of whom are young and likely to have a family. It is highly improbable that any son of mine would sit on the throne."

"These things could be made to happen, Your Highness."

"You speak of treason, My Lord."

"I speak of furthering the cause of my future wife," he responds.

The song comes to an end, saving me from answering. I dip into a curtsy, glad to be rid of the man and hoping that it's going to be the last I see of him, or hear about the prospect of marrying him. Though I fear that's not going to be the case.

"Princess, may I have this dance?"

I turn to find the younger brother of Lord Hexamble beside me.

I force a smile to my face because I'd much rather take a rest, but at least I haven't heard anything bad about him. In this man's case, his worst offence is that my heart is already spoken for by my first love, and that's hardly his fault.

"Of course, Lord..."

"Stefan if you would wish," he says as he takes my hand and starts the next dance. He isn't as practised as Lord Drewsforth, but his nervousness would be almost endearing in other circumstances.

"I'm not sure it's entirely proper, Lord Stefan."

"Perhaps not, but I would rather be on friendly terms with my wife-to-be."

I force a smile to my face. Why are they all so certain that they are the ones who will be chosen as my husband? "An admirable trait," I respond instead of voicing my question.

"And one I hope you might share. Perhaps you could come to House Hexamble's apartment at some point this week for dinner so we might get to know one another better?"

"I would have to see what my father, the King, thinks of such a proposition," I respond, not really knowing how else to.

"I understand completely, Your Highness. Just know that I plan to do my utmost to convince you, and your father, that I would be the perfect candidate to be your prince consort," Lord Stefan replies.

"Thank you, My Lord." The song comes to an end and I almost sigh with relief until I spot another of my potential suitors heading in my direction. Panic builds within me as I try to think of a reasonable way to escape without drawing too much attention.

"May I have this dance?" a familiar voice says.

I spin around, a genuine smile spreading over my face. "Of course, My Lord," I say loudly enough for anyone in the vicinity to hear so they can't tell me not to dance with him.

Hector chuckles as he takes my hand in his, the touch sending tingles through me even through my gloves.

"What are you doing here?" I ask.

"How did you know it was me?"

"I'd recognise your voice anywhere," I respond. "But that doesn't answer my question."

He moves me through the dance with a firm hand on my waist, and I enjoy it far more than with any of the others. Probably because this is someone I *want* to touch me.

"I've been briefed that your father expects a disturbance this evening, and have been instructed to cut in on any dance where I think you're exposed to danger. Though I will admit that I might have taken advantage of the vagueness of the request when I saw the expression on your face."

"I was in danger of dancing with someone I did not wish to," I respond flatly.

"You say that like it is nothing."

"It is nothing. Perhaps I have postponed the dance for this turn around the floor, or even the next one, but clearly my father is expecting me to dance with all of my potential suitors tonight."

He lets out a low growl unlike anything I've ever heard from him before. He clears his throat. "My apologies."

"None necessary," I say softly. "You know I don't want to marry any of them, right?"

"I do."

"And that there's nothing I can do about the fact I have to." My voice cracks as I say the last part. I glance down, glad I'm wearing a mask that at least partly hides my face.

"There has to be something," Hector whispers.

"I can't think of it. Everyone keeps reminding me that it's the duty of a princess to marry. Though from what I can gather, it's the duty of any vampire daughter to do just that." There's a bitterness in my voice that I don't intend to be there. "We shouldn't be talking about this here." I look around to make sure no one is paying any attention.

"Perhaps not," he responds. "But I'm here, if you want to talk about it."

I look up and meet his gaze, seeing both earnestness and pain in his eyes. It makes me want to cry. Why is the world so cruel that it wants us to forfeit what we've had together? So much so that we can't even share one moment now.

I push the thought aside as the dance comes to an end.

"If you want me to ask you to dance again, touch your necklace," Hector says softly as he bows.

I hold his gaze and reach my finger to the ruby at my throat.

He chuckles. "I didn't mean now."

"I know," I respond. "But if I could dance with you the entire night, I would."

"That would be dangerous," he responds.

"Yes."

He nods and waits for me to curtsy to him before disappearing to wherever it is he's lurking.

I watch him go, my heart aching as I realise that it doesn't matter how many suitors my father throws at me, there's only one person I'd ever consider marrying.

And he's the one I can't have.

Chapter 4

I toss and turn, sleep evading me, even though I'm exhausted after the past few days of meeting with suitors and putting up with their awful attempts to sway both me and Father. At least I'm now allowed to know who they are, though I'm not convinced I'll have a say when the time comes to draw up the final contract. Every time I try to convince Father to change his mind about this, he gives me a look that tells me he's not going to. Whether I like it or not, he's going to marry me off.

Thoughts of marrying inevitably lead me back to Hector, no matter how much I try not to. I know that the more I think about him like this, the more it's going to hurt when I'm forced down the aisle to say vows to a man I don't love. But what else am I supposed to do? He's here every day, in my room, touching my hand accidentally. Dancing with me to save me from more inane conversations with suitors. And watching me.

Always watching. It's far more than just protective, I've seen the way he watches me move and he does nothing to hide how much he wants me.

My breath catches in my throat as I think about what would happen if he did something about that. Would it be a clandestine kiss? Would he sneak into my bed?

I swallow hard just thinking about it, and without meaning to, my hand strays downwards, across my stomach and down between my legs. It's hard to tell which of my thoughts are memories, and which are hopes for what could happen right now. Hector is just outside the door, if I cry out, he'll hear me, and maybe even come inside to check that I'm all right.

If he does, he'll know exactly what I'm doing. Would he turn away? Or would he give in to desire?

Tension builds within me, but the doors of my room fly open before I can get there. I pull my hand away and sit up, using the blankets to cover me.

"You need to get up," Hector says, panic in his voice.

"What's happening?"

"Intruders in the royal rooms."

I nod and throw back the covers. His gaze rests on me for a moment, and I realise I'm only wearing a thin nightdress. "I need to get dressed..."

"No time." He grabs a robe and holds it out for me. I slip my arms into it and knot it around my waist.

He grabs hold of my hand and pulls me towards the back of the room.

"Where are we going?" I ask.

"No time," he responds, sliding open a panel in the wall and pushing me inside. He gets in with me and closes the wall behind us.

My heart pounds, but it's not all to do with fear. I can feel the heat of Hector's body radiating against mine, and smell the sweet scent of his blood as it races through his system. It's a heady combination, especially combined with the thoughts I'd been having before he entered my room, and I find my fangs lengthening without me meaning them to. I move to cover them, but my hand brushes against Hector's chest instead.

I'm caught in a trance as he captures my hand in his, lifting it up to his mouth and kissing it. Even through his closed lips I can feel that his fangs are out.

And I know exactly what that means.

I swallow hard, the sound incredibly loud in the close quarters. His eyes darken, even as I can tell he's trying to focus on the problem at hand.

Shouts come from the other side of the wall, but they're indistinguishable from everything else. What sounds like guards chasing people comes next, but as nothing seems to be happening in my room, it's impossible to tell exactly what's going on.

"What do we do now?" I ask.

"I don't know," he admits. "But you can't go back to your room alone, not until we know it's safe."

"You could come with me?"

He shakes his head. "We should go to mine. I'm not using it at the moment, it's connected to the secret passageways, and no one would expect to look for you there." He doesn't wait for me to respond and pulls me down the secret passageway. There's a draft coming from somewhere, but other than that, it's very nondescript. It's strange to think this is hidden behind the walls of the rooms I regularly frequent.

He pauses at what appears to be a peg board

and picks up a gold pin. He searches for the right spot and pushes it in.

"What is this?" I ask.

"Guard communication," he responds. "If one of the others comes to check, they'll know you're safe and accounted for. But no one else will know what it means."

"Oh." I look at the other pins, presuming they match the rest of my family. "No one else's are used yet."

"It doesn't mean anything, Agnes," he promises. "I came straight to you when I knew what was going on, we're just the first to pass the board. Now come, we should get you properly to safety."

I nod, giving one last look at the board and hoping that the rest of the guards will do what they're supposed to and protect the others.

Hector reaches for my hand and takes it in his, the warmth comforting in far more ways than it should be. He pulls me down the corridor, moving quickly but confidently.

He only slows as he comes to another section of the wall, and he slides it away to reveal a small room with a bed and not much else.

I step inside and wait until he closes it. "What's happening?"

"I don't know," he says. "But my orders are to protect you at all costs, so that's what I'm doing." He moves to the normal door and tests it, satisfied that it's locked. He pushes a dresser in front of it and then repeats the motion with the other door, ultimately barricading us in.

"So, no one knows where we are, and no one's going to look for us until the morning because they're certain you're protecting me?"

"Something like that," he agrees. "They know you're safe if they look at the board, but it's better if no one knows where you are in case the wrong person comes across the information. There are safe rooms all over the palace."

"I'm not sure I like having my life threatened, but I'm not exactly against the consequences."

He chuckles. "I should have realised as much. You should take the bed."

"No," I answer instantly. "You can't sleep on the floor."

"I'm not going to be sleeping, Agnes. I have to keep guard."

"You've been awake all day, you can't not rest."

"I'll sit with you," he says.

I take his hand and pull him over to the bed. He comes willingly, but the expression on his face says he's not thinking about sleep, even though he should be.

I don't mind in the slightest.

I undo the knot at my stomach and shrug off my robe, hanging it on a hook on the side of the wardrobe. "Which side of the bed do you want? The left still?"

"The right," he says, his voice low and gruff. "Then I'm closer to the door."

I nod and slip under the blanket. It's scratchier than the one in my room, but it isn't unpleasant. It reminds me of all the times the two of us shared a blanket before, when none of the opulence of the palace was something I even knew about.

Hector strips off his jacket and belt, but otherwise stays clothed before climbing in beside me.

His steady breathing is a welcome sound, and one I wish I heard more of.

"Do you know what I miss about being human?" I ask.

"You were never human," he points out. "Neither of us were."

"All right, do you know what I miss about thinking I was human?" I say instead, staring up at the dark ceiling and trying not to think too much about how close he is.

"The freedom?" he guesses.

"Well, yes, but that wasn't what I was thinking about. It was when it would get hot in summer, and we'd go down to the river and take off our shoes. We'd try and catch fish."

"You even managed one time," he says.

I laugh at the memory. "So I did. But I got so excited about it that I dropped it right back into the river."

"That was the day I knew I loved you," he says softly. "You were so carefree, and you looked up and smiled at me, and I knew deep in my soul that I'd never love anyone the way I loved you."

My heart skips a beat, which he can probably hear in the silence of the room. "I didn't know."

"That's because it took me months to actually kiss you."

"I remember. It was at the harvest festival. Behind the hay bales because we thought no one would notice us there. It was only a couple of years later that we learned that *everyone* went behind them to kiss." I smile at the memory. "I miss the smell of hay."

"And sunshine." He sighs wistfully. "Looking up at the sky and seeing birds instead of bats."

"It was beautiful," I agree. "And I never appreciated it as much as I should have."

"You didn't expect to get trapped in a palace of darkness." The excuse is valid, but it doesn't stop it from being just that.

"There are a lot of things I didn't expect," I respond. "I never thought I'd be separated from the love of my life, or that I'd find myself having to worry about tiaras, or court manners, or who I have to marry."

"Maybe you would have worried about that in time."

"I wouldn't have," I respond. "I knew exactly who I was going to marry."

"The butcher's son, right?" he teases.

I laugh, feeling more carefree than I have in a while. "I can't even remember his name."

"David," Hector responds. "That was his name."

"I planned on marrying you," I say softly. I don't think he needs me to spell it out, but I need to say it out loud. I need to say the thing I truly feel like I lost when I became a vampire. The dream I took for granted. "I thought we'd have a farmhouse by the river, and that's where we'd have a family and spend our days tending to chickens. Or goats. Or cows. I'm not sure, I never knew much about farm animals. You'd work in the sun, and you'd come home to a hearty stew and tales about what the little ones had been up to all day."

"It's quite a picture," he says softly.

"Yes."

"I wanted that too," he says. "Though maybe without the chickens, they scare me."

I snort without meaning to. "You're a royal bodyguard and you're scared of chickens?"

"There's not much risk of them wandering around the palace," he points out.

"How didn't I know this?"

"I'm not sure. It must have come up at some point," he says.

"Well, I promise that if there are any chickens attacking, I'll protect you."

"It's appreciated." His hand creeps across the bed and brushes across mine.

I hold my breath as I entwine our fingers together, taking his hand in mine. It's a familiar gesture between us, but it feels so much more intimate than it has before. Like this time is special.

"I don't think I mind being a vampire," I say

softly. "But if you'd asked me a couple of weeks ago, I think I'd have answered differently."

"What changed?"

"You came back into my life."

"Agnes..." Despite the pain in his voice, he doesn't pull his hand away.

"I know." I don't need him to tell me that we can't be together, I know it isn't possible. "I hate being royal."

"It's worse at the bottom of the food chain," he reminds me.

"It seems there's no real winning," I murmur. "But I was happier before I was a princess. Freer."

"I know."

I sigh. "I suppose there's nothing I can do about it though. This is what I was born to. It was either accept this or die."

"You made the right choice," Hector says. "A world without you in it wouldn't be a world I wanted to live in."

"I'm glad you're in my life again." The darkness makes it easy to tell him the truth of how I'm feeling, even if I know it's a risk to.

"Same."

We lapse into silence, and I soon feel sleep drift

over me, far more easily than when I'd been alone in the grand bed of a princess. Because despite the fact I have all those trappings, I don't need them. I would have been perfectly happy living my life with barely anything and Hector by my side.

Chapter 5

Sleep fades away as I turn and find myself face-to-face with Hector. Even in the dark, it's easy to make his features. My heart aches at the thought that this night is just our one stolen moment. Something we can share that no one knows about, but it's all we can actually have. There's nothing more after this.

I lean in to kiss his cheek, but he moves at the last second and his lips meet mine instead. I'm surprised when he kisses me back, but in a good way. It's tentative at first, but then everything seems to click into place and the kiss turns demanding and full of need. I feel my own desire rising within me and I know I won't be satisfied until I'm with him in every way.

"I've dreamt of this," I murmur as I break the

kiss. "Every night since you came back into my life." I lean forward and kiss his neck, feeling his breathing turn shallow as I graze my teeth against his pulse point. I've never wanted to do that to anyone before, but with Hector, the urge is there to bite.

"Agnes." My name is half-groan when it comes from his lips.

"Yes?"

"We shouldn't."

"Do you want to?" I ask.

"More than anything." His gaze meets mine and I can see the truth of what he's saying in his eyes. "But we shouldn't."

"Why not?"

"Because you're a princess, and I'm a nobody."

"You're not a nobody to me," I whisper. "You never have been."

"You're supposed to be getting married soon," he says.

"Doesn't that mean I should take my pleasure while I can still get it?" I ask. "And if you're worried about my future husband discovering I'm not a virgin, then I should remind you of a night about six years ago, there was wine, and a picnic, and only the stars as our witnesses. It was perfect.

Far more perfect than any wedding night could be."

"In another world, if we'd been married, I would have made our wedding night perfect," he promises. "I just wish I could do that in this one."

"You can make tonight perfect," I whisper.

"Someone broke into the royal apartments tonight."

"And it means I get to spend time with you away from prying eyes and in a bed that means I have to be pressed tightly against you," I respond, shuffling closer as if to illustrate my point.

Hector groans. "You have no idea how much I want you, Agnes."

A knowing smile crosses my face. "I can guess. It's hard to hide in a small bed."

He clears his throat. "You should be glad I'm able to hold a conversation."

"I'd be just as happy if you held me," I respond.

He reaches out and touches my face. My eyes flutter closed at his touch, reminding me of all of the times we've done this before, the sweet moments and the whispered promises.

Before we realised that our life would be something other than what we expected.

"Hector." I don't say anything else. I don't know

what *to* say, I just know that I want him with every fibre of my being.

His lips brush against mine and I respond immediately. It's a sweet kiss despite the situation, and one that tells me a lot about how he feels.

I deepen it, wanting more. He doesn't protest and his hand trails down until it's on my waist. The fabric of my nightdress does nothing to dampen the heat I can feel from his touch and I long to feel it against my bare skin.

I put my hand over his and move it downwards until it's at the bottom of my nightdress. I let go, intending to give him an out if he really doesn't want this.

He pulls back, and for a moment, I think he's putting an end to the situation, but then he pulls his shirt over his head, and I know he's just as lost as I am.

I sit up, the blankets falling away as I do. I pull my nightdress over my head and throw it to the floor, leaving me exposed to the cool air of the room and the scorching gaze of the man in bed with me. The darkness does nothing to hide any of it from us.

He cups my cheek in his hand and draws me to him, kissing me hungrily. My hands trace over his chest, the muscles there far more defined than the last time I saw him naked. But despite how much has happened in the past four years, I can tell who he is hasn't changed. He's still the dependable Hector he's always been.

He pushes me back down onto the bed and breaks the kiss, trailing kisses down my neck, paying particular attention to the spot where my pulse pounds. Now I think about it, I can hear his blood racing too, and I can smell the change that has come over it now we're giving in to what we want. Maybe that's my imagination, but it isn't something to think about much now.

His tongue grazes over my nipple and I let out a gasp, arching into him. Despite the time that has passed, he hasn't forgotten what I like, and that only drives my desire higher. There's a part of me that wants to hurry him, but the rest is determined to enjoy the pace he's setting.

We have all night before he has to return me to my room.

His breath tickles against my stomach as he moves further down, using a strong hand to move my leg into a better position, baring me to him.

My lips part as a gasp escapes me. He's barely touching me and I already feel as if I'm about to explode. Slowly, he leans in and presses a kiss against the inside of my knee. My hands bunch into the blanket as he moves higher, tracing patterns on my skin using his tongue. All thoughts of anything other than the way it feels to have him touch me like this are gone, and I can barely even remember where we are.

He settles between my legs and looks up at me, his gaze locking with mine. Even through the haze of desire, I can see a lot of unspoken words in his eyes. He wants me, but it's about much more than just this moment, even if neither of us can admit as much.

My head tips back as he leans in and uses his tongue, the precision of every movement causing my desire to curl up within me tighter and tighter. My fingers tangle in his hair, which only seems to encourage him and he picks up the pace. Unintelligible sounds spill from my lips as I urge him on until my whole body begins to shake and the world disappears, the only thing I can focus on is Hector's touch and the pleasure it brings me.

A loud moan escapes me and I close my legs around his head, but he doesn't stop until I'm completely pushed over the edge.

I flop back against the pillow and tug on his hair

so he knows I'm spent. He shifts and comes to join me, a lazy and satisfied smile on his face.

"I've been thinking about doing that since the moment I took my position as your guard," he says in a low gruff voice.

"I've been thinking about you doing it for just as long," I murmur in response. "You certainly haven't forgotten what you're doing."

He chuckles. "I had a good teacher."

I snort. "More like we worked it out together. Those first few times were a lot more fumbly."

"Mmm, but once we found all the right ways to please each other, it was a lot of fun," he responds.

"It was." I reach out and touch his chest. "And I remember a lot more of it."

"Is that so?"

"Mmhmm." I push myself up off the bed and straddle him, feeling the need already starting to grow inside me again. "I remember that you liked it when you could see me." I reach down between us and take his hardness in my hand so I can guide him to my entrance.

"I do like that," he says, his voice raspy and full of desire.

A whimper escapes me as I sink down onto him.

How have I managed to wait this long to feel this again?

Hector puts a hand on my hip as I move back and forth, breathing heavily and needing more of this. More of *him*. The pleasure is making everything a bit hazy and I lose the steady pace, lost in how good it feels to be with him.

"Let me," he murmurs, flipping us over so I'm on my back.

I wrap my legs around his waist and he pushes in deeper, causing a long moan to break free from me. He kisses my neck, the points of his fangs brushing over the soft skin of my neck and giving me a new desire.

"Bite me," I murmur.

There's no hesitation as his fangs sink into me. I've never been drunk from before, but the feeling is a heady one, and it heightens all of the other sensations going on in my body right now. I can feel my release building within me, every touch from Hector almost threatening to send me over the edge.

He removes his fangs and gently traces the edges of the twin wounds on my neck with his tongue, only putting me more on edge. I dig my fingers into his back, urging him on, needing more.

"Hector..."

He starts to lose focus, and I know he's close to the edge. I tighten my legs around him, drawing him deeper still. He lets out a groan and pushes away from me before finding release.

I frown and look at him. "What..."

"We can't have a baby from this."

Understanding dawns on me. "It's not easy for vampires to get pregnant," I assure him.

"It's still too much of a risk to take."

I nod and shuffle up in the bed, reaching out to take his hard length in my hand, stroking slowly. "That's the sensible decision," I say. "But it doesn't mean you shouldn't have your fun too."

He reaches out and guides my face to his so he can kiss me while I continue to touch him. His body stills and he pulses in my hand as he finally finds his release.

My fangs poke against my lips as I look at him, my whole body tingling with satisfaction.

"We should clean up," he says, getting to his feet and heading over to the wash basin in the corner of the room. "The water's cold, I'm afraid." He dips a cloth in and brings it back to me so I can clean myself.

"Worth it," I respond. "Especially now I get to properly fall asleep in your arms,"

He laughs. "Weren't you already doing that?"

"Sleeping in the same bed as you is different from sleeping *with* you," I point out.

"Mmm." He takes the cloth back to the wash basin and drops it by the side before coming back to bed.

He wraps his arms around me and I nestle into him, enjoying the smell that is only him.

"If I'm sleeping with you, then there's fun to be had in the middle of the night," I muse.

"How did I forget how insatiable you are?" He kisses the top of my head.

"Only with you," I whisper, turning around in his arms so we're face to face. "There's been no one since I got here."

"Because you've been guarded the whole time?"

"Because I never stopped loving you, Hector." I meet his gaze, hoping he can see the truth of my words on my face. "After I got over the shock of the Golden Moon, I spent the whole night crying. Partly because of what I'd seen, but also because I thought of you waiting for me the next day and me just not showing up. I tried to send a letter, but I have no idea if it was ever delivered."

"Me neither," he says.

"Right, because you weren't there."

"No. I was taken the night of the Golden Moon and was given a choice, I could become a servant, or I could train intensely for three years to become a royal guard. It was only in the morning when someone stopped me from going outside that I realised it meant I'd never get to see you again."

"Until you walked into my room a couple of weeks ago." I trace patterns over his chest.

"Yes."

"How..." I swallow hard. "How did you get assigned to me?"

"It's drawn by lot," he says. "They have your next five sworn guards picked out. The job isn't a safe one and they assume that most guards will die within a few years."

"Hector..."

"I don't plan on dying," he promises, smoothing a hand over my cheek. "Not now. Before, I didn't think I cared. I've thought about you constantly for the past four years. Some of it was guilt for the fact I left you, even though I didn't have any choice, and part of it was worry over what would become of you. And the rest of it..." he trails off.

"The rest?"

"Longing," he says. "To see you again, to hold you. To know that you were all right."

I touch his face. "I'm all right tonight."

He kisses my fingers as they brush against his lips.

"Tonight isn't going to be enough." My admission is almost too quiet to hear, but I know he's heard it.

"I know."

"Father could have you killed for it." I don't like that it's true, but it's definitely something for him to consider if he wants to do this again. I don't want him unnecessarily in danger for me.

He surprises me by laughing. "Your father could have me killed for dozens of reasons, none of which would be as worth it as this."

I want to protest, but I know he's right.

"The life expectancy of a royal guard isn't particularly high," he says.

"I don't want you to die."

"Believe me, I'm going to do everything I can not to." He lifts my hand to his lips and kisses it.

"As will I."

"Except not sleep with me," he jokes.

"I don't want to just sleep with you," I admit. "I want more than that."

"We can't have more, Agnes."

Tears prick at the corners of my eyes and I

nuzzle into his chest, not wanting him to see them. "There must be a way."

"If there is, I don't know of one," he responds.

"We'll find it," I respond, a certainty in my voice that I don't know if I actually feel. But one thing is for certain, now I've found Hector again, I don't intend to let him out of my life again.

Chapter 6

My bedroom door opens and a smile springs to my face as Hector walks inside. It's only been a couple of hours since we said goodbye in his room, but it's still too long.

He checks behind him and closes the door, leaving us alone unless I call for the maid.

Without waiting a single moment, I head over to him, wrapping my arms around his neck and sinking into him. He kisses me deeply.

"I take it there are no regrets about last night?" he asks as he strokes a thumb across my cheek.

"One," I admit.

He raises an eyebrow. "That it ended?"

"No, actually. It's that I never got to drink from you," I respond, touching my neck where his fangs pierced me. The marks are already gone, but I'm never going to be able to forget the way it felt for his teeth to pierce through my skin and for me to share that part of myself with him. It's almost more intimate than the rest of what we did.

"Next time," he promises.

"So you're not going to tell me it's foolish for us to try and be together now we're in the cold light of day?" I ask.

He chuckles. "It is foolish. And we're being fools for not listening to our heads, but I don't want to stay away from you, Agnes."

"Good." I lean in to kiss him again but the click of the doors has me jumping away.

Hector clears his throat. "I've done a check on all of the entry points to your rooms, Princess," he says loudly.

"Thank you," I respond, feeling a little flustered.

Maude steps inside. "Excuse the intrusion, Your Highness, but His Majesty, the King, is here and asking for an audience."

"Oh, I see." My voice shakes as I respond, which isn't a good thing. "Please send him in."

Hector looks a little panicked and I long to tell him that it's going to be fine, but I don't want to risk saying anything that could reveal what's between us.

My father strides into the room looking surprisingly well-rested considering what occurred last night.

"Daughter," he says stoically. "We should speak about yesterday."

I resist the urge to look at Hector. How can Father possibly know what happened between us?

I swallow hard. "What about it?"

"There is concern amongst the guards about how easily intruders got into our space. We're going to be increasing security. You are to keep your guard with you at all times."

"I am?" I try not to let my relief be too obvious. If he's ordering Hector to stay with me more, then he certainly doesn't suspect that we slept together.

"Everywhere you go, Agnes. I'm serious about this. We can't have anything happening to you before the marriage contracts are signed."

But after that is fine. I push away the thought. "Are you still going ahead with that?" I blurt out.

"Why would I not? Our House must be protected, and the best way to do that is through an alliance. You will marry the man who brings the biggest advantage to us."

"Not the one I like the most?"

"Your opinion in this is irrelevant," he says firmly.

"But should it be? This is my life, Father..."

"And I am your *King*."

I flinch at the anger in his voice.

"You do not get to tell me how best to rule my kingdom," he says. "There are more people depending on us than you can even imagine, and I am the one responsible for all of them. Your only job is to marry where I tell you to. Do you understand?"

My heart races, and I'm pretty sure he can tell as much. "Yes, Father," I murmur, bowing my head.

"Good." He nods stiffly, his anger already fading. He turns to look at Hector. "Thank you for protecting my daughter last night."

Hector bows deeply, seeming a little shaky. "The honour was all mine, Your Majesty."

"See that you continue to care for her with the same devotion," he commands.

"Always." Hector's gaze slips to me, making my heart skip a beat.

I hope my father can't hear and start asking questions. Though he probably thinks it's still all down to fear, which in part it is. I haven't often seen him like this, and I can't say I particularly like it.

"Very good." He nods a couple of times and strides out of the room.

I wait a few moments before heading to the doors. "See that I'm not disturbed, please," I say to Maude, my voice shaking. "Last night was exhausting." Mostly because Hector and I woke several more times and couldn't stop our hands from wandering, but she doesn't need to know that. Everyone will just assume that I mean because of the intruders.

"Of course, Your Highness. I'll be here if you need anything."

"Thank you." I give her what I hope is a friendly smile before shutting the doors.

I lean back against the door and take a few deep breaths, trying to collect myself and put the intensity of Father's reaction out of my mind.

Hector pulls me into his arms and I rest my head against his chest. His scent is almost as soothing as the hand he's rubbing up and down my back.

"Are you all right?" he asks.

"I will be," I whisper. "I'm here with you."

"Don't you think your maid will grow suspicious of me being here alone with you?" Hector asks.

"She'll just have overheard Father commanding

me to keep you with me. I'm simply being a dutiful princess and taking him at his word." Bitterness seeps into my tone. "I'm nothing but a pawn to him."

"I'm sure that's not true," Hector responds, but I can hear the doubt in his voice.

"It's fine." I push away from him and steady myself. "I'll just do what I can to play the dutiful princess and find another way out of this marriage."

He nods.

"Perhaps I should ask Maude to bring your bed into my bedchamber," I muse.

"Agnes! You can't do that."

"I know," I say with a sigh. "I just hate it. None of the vampires care about chastity, but I still can't take a lover. It makes no sense."

"You're the princess," he points out. "I don't think it has to make sense for them."

"I'd give up being a princess for you. If Father told me I could do that, then I would."

"Even if it would mean a life of poverty and potentially exile?" he asks, stepping closer.

"Yes. Especially then." I wrap my arms around his neck. "It wouldn't be easy, I'm not going to pretend otherwise, but there would be no one to worry about. No suitors to placate, no court politics to play. It would just be the two of us facing whatever life throws at us."

"It sounds idyllic," he murmurs.

"But impossible."

"Yes." He rubs a hand up and down my back. "But that's not going to stop me from loving you. I've missed you every day for the past four years. I'm not about to let another go by."

"Me neither," I agree, leaning in to kiss him, putting all of my emotions into the moment. I hate that this is where we've come to, but I know lamenting it isn't going to get us anywhere.

Even so, I'm not ready to let go of my dream of this being more than just a fleeting thing before my father marries me off. I'm going to find a way to make a future with Hector my reality.

Chapter 7

The dining table is as tense as it normally is when we're called to family dinner. The Queen sits at the foot of the table, glaring at me in distaste, clearly wishing I wasn't here, while being glad that Lincoln is not. I'm not even sure *where* he is, but he seems to have been successfully getting out of most of the family engagements we've been called to.

Father sits at the head of the table, gesturing to the servants to bring him more wine, food, and blood, while Marcus and I sit mostly in silence, knowing that there's not much we can do to break through the tension.

I don't know why Father insists on us having these dinners, he must be aware of how little all of us want to be here. I look up and meet Hector's gaze, but he's careful not to break his neutral expression while there are so many other people around. I don't blame him, the consequences of our relationship coming out in the open here could be dire.

All of the other guards in the room are standing with the same stoicism. One each for Marcus and his mother, two for our father.

"You," the Queen says, snapping her fingers at Hector.

"Your Majesty," he says with a dip of his head.

"Fetch me some wine."

"Hector is my sworn shield, Your Majesty," I say. "He's not a servant."

"Of course he's a servant. What do you think a guard is?" she says without looking at me. "Well? Are you going to get me some wine?"

"Your Majesty," Hector says with a dip of his head.

I ball my hand up in the fabric of my dress, wishing I could interfere further and tell her to stop talking to him like that, but I think better of it. I can't have any of them know how much affection I hold for him or it'll raise questions.

I watch Hector leave, hating that he's no longer

in the room. It feels like I have less protection now, even though that's probably not true.

Dinner continues as if the interruption hadn't happened, and it's only a few minutes until Hector returns with a new pitcher of wine. He pours a glass for the Queen and hovers.

"Would you like me to fill your glass, Princess?" he asks.

I meet his gaze and pick up my glass, holding it out to him. "That would be most kind."

He takes it from me, his fingers brushing against mine as he does, sending tingles across my skin. I know it's dangerous for us to even have a fleeting moment like this when there are others in the room, but it doesn't stop either of us.

Hector hands my glass back to me and sets the pitcher of wine on the table before returning to his place by the wall.

From the other side of the table, Marcus gives me a curious look, but I avoid his gaze. He can speculate all he wants, but I'm not going to reveal anything.

"You'll be pleased to know that the contract for your upcoming marriage is almost finalised, Agnes," Father says.

My fork clatters against my plate as I drop it. "It

is?" I glance in Hector's direction again and see the tick of his jaw at the mention of it. I wish I could tell him it's going to be fine, but I don't know how to with so many people around.

"The only thing left is to decide which of the three potential suitors is the best for the future of House Soveguine," he says.

"Do I..." I trail off and swallow down any protest about which would be the best for *me*. It's perfectly clear to me that isn't even a consideration in the conversation and nothing I can say is going to change that. The best I can do is not draw attention to myself and hope that I can find a way out of the situation before it's too late.

"I thought there were five candidates?" Marcus asks.

I cover my surprise that he's been cut out of the negotiations.

Father makes a dismissive noise. "The offer from Lord Fallmartin was never truly a contender."

A satisfied smile crosses the Queen's face. Presumably, she's happy I won't be marrying into her House.

"With all of the current unrest, we can't wait a year for Agnes to be married. The sooner she's under the protection of her husband, the sooner we can reassign her guard," Father says.

I squeak.

He turns his attention to me and looks expectantly at me to continue speaking.

I clear my throat. "I thought I might take my sword shield with me when I marry," I say, not looking at Hector as I do. It's not something I've thought about until now. "I've become used to him."

Father sighs. "I suppose I can make that a stipulation in your marriage contract should you wish it. You are my daughter, and he has proved loyal to you."

I nod and look down at my plate. "That is appreciated. I'd much rather have someone I know beside me as a protector rather than a stranger."

"Then it shall be done," Father says, surprising me with how easily he's caved to the request.

"Who is the other suitor you've dismissed?" Marcus asks between bites of food.

"Lord Hexamble's younger brother. He isn't the heir to his House, and he doesn't have a title of his own, hardly a suitable match for a princess," Father says.

My fingers tighten around my knife to the point

that I nick the skin of my finger against my thumb. I set it down and put my thumb to my mouth to ease the sting of the cut. At least the injury gives me a reason to have tears in my eyes, but Father's words are cutting into me far deeper than any knife can. They're a reminder that what I want can't be had.

"I'm surprised you haven't dismissed the suit of Lord Falgrove yet," Marcus says. "Considering he's already married, I don't see him as a good fit."

I flash my brother an appreciative smile even while I'm still struggling internally. At least he's trying to protect me from someone who is likely to try and hurt me. Somehow, I doubt the fact I'm a princess is going to protect me against someone for whom cruelty is in their nature.

"Lord Falgrove is the richest of the candidates," Father responds. "That is not to be dismissed easily. Powerful Houses aligned with the throne are to be desired, and enemies to be avoided."

"I've heard that his wife is no longer a problem," the Queen says, a twisted smile pulling at her lips.

I turn to her and she gives me a look that says she knows exactly what the problem with Lord Falgrove is, and she plans on doing nothing to avert my fate.

"Is that so?" Father asks, a curious expression on his face. "Then I should speak with him tomorrow."

"Surely there should be a mourning period?" I blurt out, panic filling me as I remember the man I danced with. I should have reported his treason when he first said it. "For his wife?"

"I suppose that's true," Father says. "Though it would not delay things further than taking Lord Fallmartin's offer."

My heart sinks and horror fills me. He has every intention of marrying me off to Lord Falgrove, I can hear it in the way he's speaking.

But I can't let this happen. There has to be some way out of this, because I can't marry a man who has killed his wife just for a chance to be royalty, because that kind of husband won't hesitate to kill me the moment he thinks it suits him better to have me dead. And with how Father is currently acting, I'm not convinced he'll even care.

Chapter 8

I head through the palace, ignoring the other members of the court until I get to the library. If my brother isn't in his rooms, then this is where he's going to be.

Hector trails behind me, on alert for anything that could cause danger. It's partly because it's his job, but I also know that he's doing it because his feelings are genuine.

One of the librarians appears to the left and I gesture for them to stop.

"Your Highness," he says with a deep bow.

"Do you know where Prince Lincoln is?" I ask.

"He's in one of the private reading rooms on the third floor, Princess."

"Thank you." I give him a tight smile while inwardly cursing my brother for the number of stairs I now have to climb. I gesture for Hector to follow me, wishing I could be more polite but knowing that there are too many possible witnesses and I can't risk it.

I pull my dress out of the way as I begin my ascent. The stairs are narrow, and not at all designed for court dresses. Whoever designed them probably didn't think the women at the palace would spend much time here.

It's a relief when I get to the top and I check Hector to make sure he's all right. He gives me a firm nod, not seeming in the slightest bit winded from the climb. Perhaps his training has helped him in that regard.

"Where are the reading rooms?" he asks.

"At the back there." It's quiet up here, and despite the climb, I can understand why Lincoln wants to be here. There aren't even any of the librarians about, giving it a sense of calm and quiet that couldn't be got otherwise.

I sigh with relief when I spot a guard dressed the same way as Hector standing outside one of the doors.

I nod to him as I pass, but he doesn't make a move to stop me.

"I'm fine, Eric," Linc says without looking up from his book.

"It's me," I say.

My brother looks up sharply. "Agnes."

"So you do remember who I am," I muse. "You've been missing from so many events recently that I was starting to worry you'd forgotten."

He chuckles. "I've known you my whole life, sister. I'm not about to forget you. Did you simply come to find me to make sure of that?"

"No, I need to talk to you. Privately. Is it safe here?"

He nods. "Your guard can wait out...Hector?" The surprise on Lincoln's face is to be expected.

"It's been a while, Linc." He clears his throat. "I mean, Your Highness."

"Don't bother with that," my brother dismisses. "Not when there's no one else around. Eric won't be able to hear me in here, but you should know that he checks in on me every ten minutes."

I frown. "Why?"

Lincoln grimaces. "Father thinks I might do something stupid like go for a walk while the sun is shining. Apparently it's common enough in newly turned dhampirs that they have guards trained to look for the signs." He rolls his eyes. "That's why I haven't been at most of the events. He thinks I'll manage to slip away during one of them."

"You're not going to, are you?" Worry fills me for my brother.

"I don't think so," he responds, sitting back in his chair but ignoring his book. At least he seems to have decided Hector can be trusted. "Sometimes it's an appealing thought. Others, not so much. I'd rather find some kind of cure to all of this."

"Do you think that's possible?" I ask, looking at Hector and feeling a sense of hope within me. If we were human, no one would care what we did.

"Nothing I've found suggests it is," he responds. "Though I'm not about to stop looking. What is it that has you so keen to escape?"

"Marriage."

He raises an eyebrow. "To someone in particular?"

"To an old man."

"We're vampires, Nes, no one is really old," Lincoln responds.

"You're supposed to be commiserating with me.

What's your plan when Father comes and tells you it's time for you to have a wife?"

"I don't plan on getting married. Marcus is the heir, it's something for him to worry about."

"Which is your prerogative because you're a *boy*." I sit down opposite him. "None of Father's choices are acceptable."

"Would they ever be?" His gaze slips to Hector, who has a serious expression on his face like he wants to say a lot of things but is keeping quiet about them.

I sigh. "No, I suppose not."

"I see." Lincoln leans back in his seat. "I can think of one way you could get around Father marrying you off."

"Oh?" I shift forward on my seat.

"Get married before he can make you."

His idea is an intriguing one, even if it does have some obvious drawbacks.

"That seems dangerous. Whoever I chose as my husband would be putting his life on the line just by agreeing," I say.

"Indeed." Lincoln looks at Hector. "If only there were someone who loved you that much."

"You don't know what you're talking about," I mutter.

Lincoln chuckles. "You've never been good at keeping your thoughts to yourself," he says to Hector.

He shuffles from side to side. "I would do anything to keep Agnes safe."

"See, he's not even pretending and calling you princess," Linc points out.

"You're not helping," I tell my brother.

He shrugs. "Or am I? If you don't want to be married to a stranger, then get married to someone else. Even Father isn't going to try and undo a marriage that's already been confirmed."

"It's dangerous. For Hector, and for me."

"Yes," Lincoln agrees. "But if it's what you want, I'll help."

"How when you're under guard all the time?" I nod towards the door.

"The secret passageways around the palace are rather interesting, don't you think?" His lips quirk up into a smile. "And where there's a will, there's a way."

I look at Hector, my heart doing funny things as I think about what it would be like to be married to him. To escape from everything that's being forced on me *and* to be with someone I love.

But I don't know if I can go through with it

knowing how much danger he's going to be in. Father could easily make me eligible to be married again simply by killing him.

Ultimately, the choice isn't really mine. He's the one whose life is on the line, so he's the one who gets to choose.

Chapter 9

There's something peaceful about being shut in my bed chamber when I know nobody else will enter. A few well-placed comments about how scared I am after the intruders broke in and no one has even thought twice about the fact I asked Hector to stay here with me. If anything, they were encouraging him. Though I suspect that's because they think he'll be sleeping at the end of my bed rather than *in* it.

A candle flickers on my bedside table, illuminating Hector's face and complementing the warmth that's always there when I look at him. I rest my head against his shoulder and trail my fingers over his chest, tracing patterns that don't mean anything as I contemplate the way my life has changed over the past few weeks. I'm glad to have Hector with me, but there's no doubt that things are a lot more complicated now.

And I don't know what to do about that. I can't marry any of the men Father has selected for me, especially not one who is known for treating his wives so badly, but Linc's idea for me to marry someone else is reckless at best. even if it works, it's going to have long-reaching consequences, and not just for me either. My entire family could suffer for it. And while there's not really any love lost between me and my father right now, I don't wish for things to get worse for my brothers.

"Are you thinking about what Linc said?" Hector asks softly.

I bite my lip and nod. "And what Father did when I saw him earlier."

"When he dismissed me?" he checks.

I nod. "I don't know if he thought you wouldn't like what he had to say, or if he just wasn't ready for anyone outside the family to know."

"Dare I ask what he said?"

I take a deep breath. He's not going to like it any more than I did when Father told me. "He's moving forward with the betrothal contract to Lord Falgrove." A shiver runs down my spine.

Hector pulls me closer and I sink into the comfort he's offering. This would be so much worse if he wasn't here.

"I know he sees it as my duty to marry for the good of the House, but surely he doesn't want to hand me over to someone who is known to be cruel to his wives? And I know no one is going to be able to prove that he killed the last one, but isn't it suspicious that he was pursuing me and then she died?"

"It does seem as if someone wanted her out of the way," Hector agrees. "It might not have been Lord Falgrove himself. There are other people with motive."

"I know." I nestle into his chest. "I don't want to live my life worrying if he's going to have me killed every time I put a foot wrong." Given the level of scheming he's already been doing, I wouldn't be surprised if part of his plan is to wed me, wait until I have a son, and then kill me along with my family so he can be the regent.

"Then marry me," Hector says softly.

I shift in the bed, the blanket falls away from me, but I barely notice, and with his eyes trained on my face, neither does he.

"It's dangerous," I respond.

"So is you being married to someone with the

ability to kill you at every turn. I don't want you to live like that, Agnes." He cups my cheek in his hand, the intensity of his gaze revealing how serious he is. "And on a more selfish note, I don't want to see you married to another man either."

"Father could kill you."

"But he might not," he responds. "Especially not if we make a home away from court."

I bite my bottom lip. "Do you think that might be possible?"

"Give me three days," he says. "Stall the betrothal so nothing is signed before that and tell your brother that we need him as a witness. Even if your father is angry, he won't hurt his son, not while your older brother is unmarried and without an heir of his own, which gives Linc plenty of time to earn forgiveness. Lincoln being our witness will make our marriage indisputable."

"You really want to do this?" I ask.

"I've thought about marrying you many times, Agnes. For longer than you can imagine possible. This isn't quite how I imagined it would happen..."

"A little less bitey?" I joke.

The sound of his chuckle vibrates through me and fills me with hope. "And with a little less threat of death."

He touches my cheek with his hand. I close my eyes and lean into his touch.

"It doesn't matter how," he promises. "All that matters is that it's happening and I'm going to do everything in my power to protect you. If you say yes."

I open my eyes and study his handsome face. "Did I not already?"

"You started worrying about me instead. Which I suppose could be interpreted as a yes."

I laugh. "It is one," I promise. "I want nothing more than to be your wife. And not just because it saves me from Father's plotting."

"Though that is an added advantage." He trails a hand down my back, sending a pleasant shiver through me.

"It is. But by royal standards, we're going about this all wrong," I muse.

"You mean I'm not supposed to ask for your hand in marriage while I'm supposed to be guarding you?"

"You are guarding me," I point out. "You're paying very close attention to me."

His hand slips under the blanket to rest on my hip. "I'm not sure this is what your father had in mind when he assigned me to be your sworn shield."

"Then he should have checked that we didn't have a history together before assigning you to me. This is all on him."

Hector chuckles. "That's one way of looking at it. But I'm not sure he'd feel the same way."

"Probably not. But I can think of many more things I'd rather think about than my father right now."

"Oh?"

I lick my lips but don't say anything as I place a hand on his chest and trail it down tantalisingly slowly while I hold his gaze.

Hector's eyes darken with desire as my hand travels lower still and, hopefully, most of his thoughts flee from his mind. I lean in and press my lips against his, knowing exactly how to celebrate our agreement to marry.

Chapter 10

I should be more nervous about sneaking out of the palace with a bag packed full of my most important belongings and as much money and gold as I could squirrel away without anyone thinking anything suspicious, but I don't. If anything, that only underlines how right this whole thing feels.

I dip through the trees and make my way to the clearing where weddings are normally held. Stones stand in a circle, weathered from the elements. They've probably seen thousands of unions, and I doubt ours is going to be the first secret ceremony held in this place.

"There you are," Linc says, making me jump.

"Sorry," I murmur. "I thought I wasn't nervous, but apparently I am."

"I'd be surprised if you weren't," he responds. "This is a big thing you're doing."

"Do you think it's the right one?"

"Only you can answer that, Nes," he says. "But I know Hector loves you and that he'll do everything he can to protect you."

"That might not be enough when Father hears about this."

My brother smiles, almost seeming properly like himself. "I wouldn't worry about that, I'll deal with it."

"I don't want you to get into trouble for me."

"Maybe this will finally convince Father that I'm a rubbish spare heir and he'll send me away or something. I wouldn't mind that. The only downside is that I'm going to miss you."

"Likewise. But you can come visit, if you want?"

He nods. "I'd like that."

"And if you ever need to get away from court, or find yourself with a potential runaway bride, my door is always open to you, brother," I say.

"I'm never going to marry, so that last one is going to be difficult," he jokes. "But I appreciate the offer all the same."

I take his hand in mine and give it a squeeze.

Hector appears before either of us can say

anything, setting down a bag that looks full of something. I lean in and kiss his cheek, glad he's here, but not in the slightest bit surprised. I never doubted he'd come.

"Are you sure you want to do this?" I ask him, wanting to give him one last chance to get out of it. I don't think he's going to say no, but I need to give him a chance to.

"I want this," he says.

"All right, then, shall we?" Lincoln asks, gesturing towards the stone altar. "It's probably better if we get this over with so you're safely away before the sun rises."

I nod and make my way there. I never expected my wedding day to look like this, but I'm happy about it all the same.

Lincoln stands in front of us, the witness to the union that can't be undone.

I look at Hector, not feeling any of the nerves I'm expecting. This is the right thing to do. Not just to free me from my father's plans to marry me off to the highest bidder, but also for me, in my heart.

The clouds clear from in front of the moon, letting the light shine down on us. I close my eyes and let the magic fill me. I'm not sure what it is about the moon that's sacred to vampires, but it seems to be connected to us. And right now, that's in my favour. A marriage made under the light of the moon and with a bond of blood can't be undone by anyone. Even a king.

My fangs descend and I lift my wrist to my mouth, biting through the skin there until my blood wells up. I hold it out to Hector, meeting his gaze.

"I offer you my blood as a symbol of this union," I say, my voice ringing out firmly.

"I accept it." His fingers close around my wrist as he raises it to his mouth and drinks some of my blood, the familiar tugging of him taking it and sending a small thrill through me.

He breaks away and kisses each of the tiny puncture marks before letting go of my arm. He bites into his own wrist and the scent of his blood fills the air, making my mouth water and the need to drink fill every part of me.

"I offer you my blood as a symbol of this union," he says, holding out his arm. The moonlight glistens off the droplets of blood and I take his arm in my hands eagerly.

His blood tastes sweet, even sweeter than usual, and I drink it down swiftly. My whole body is buzzing with some kind of feeling, though I think it's just my imagination. Tonight is going to be special to me for the rest of my unnaturally long life, that's what this feeling is.

I pull back and trace my tongue around the wounds in his wrist. I'm not sure if it actually helps with the healing process, but there have never been any visible marks left the other times we've bitten each other, so I have to assume so.

"What the moon has made cannot be undone," Lincoln says. "You may go forth from this place, united as one." He gives each of us a nod.

A giddy feeling fills me and I realise that this is it. I'm married, and not to someone of Father's choice either, but of my own. I look up at Hector and find him smiling widely, clearly experiencing some of the same feelings I am.

"All right, it's done," Lincoln says, clearing his throat. "Congratulations to you both. But you should get going, there are only a few hours until dawn and I don't need to tell you what will happen if you're not inside before then."

"We know," Hector responds.

My brother pulls me into an embrace. "Best of luck, sister."

"And to you. Remember my offer."

"Always." He breaks away and offers Hector a firm handshake. "Now I'm going to go and make sure my guards don't notice I'm missing." He waves and heads back up to the castle.

"We should get going," I say. "I know he's not going to tell anyone, but the longer we're here, the greater the risk becomes that someone will find out anyway."

"I know. But before we go, there's something I need to do," Hector says.

"Oh?"

"I need to kiss my wife."

My heart flutters in response and I step closer to him even as he reaches out for me. My eyes flutter closed as he leans in and presses his lips against mine.

I run my fingers through his hair and push my body against his, feeling the heat of him despite the cool air of the world around us. I wish we had more time to truly enjoy one another now that the deed is done, but consummating our marriage is going to have to wait until we're safely at our destination.

We break apart and Hector smooths a thumb over my cheek. "I love you, Agnes," he whispers.

"I love you too," I respond.

"And now we really should go." He picks up his bag and takes my hand in his, pulling me through the trees until we come to a pair of tethered horses.

"How..."

"Your brother gave me some money and jokingly called it a dowry. I'm not sure where he got it from, but given the situation, I thought it was best not to ask. You know how to ride?"

I nod. "Father insisted I learned once I came here."

"Good." He holds out his hands to help me mount and I throw my leg over one of the saddles. My dress isn't designed for riding and bunches up around my upper legs.

Hector passes up my bag to me and I secure it in place behind me.

"Where are we going?" I ask once he's seated on his own horse.

"To a small castle down by the river. It's got a farm attached, but I'm not sure how much we'll be able to work it considering we can't go out during the day. Linc managed to get a message to my mother and she's made it ready for us. We'll still have to rely on your brother for blood and some supplies, but we should be self-sufficient when it comes to food."

"A castle by the river sounds a little grander than a farm," I muse.

"Well, I am married to a princess," he jokes.

I laugh and smile at him as we set off through the woods, riding at a steady but unhurried pace. No one is going to know we're gone for several hours at least, giving us plenty of time to get to our castle before anyone comes looking for us.

Which means that we've successfully managed to avert the worst, and I get to spend my days married to someone I love without having to endure a life of politics and my father's choices.

Epilogue

I glance longingly at the boarded-up window, wishing it didn't have to be that way, but we couldn't risk daylight getting into the castle, which meant all of the windows had been covered. I have no idea how Hector managed to achieve all of this in three days, but I suspect I'll come to learn about that in time.

The scent of freshly baked bread fills the air, and I find myself grateful that my mother thought to teach me these skills as well as those she deemed necessary for a princess.

Carefully, I pull the loaf out of the oven and set it aside to cool.

A knock on the door draws my attention and I head to open it, surprised to find Hector's mother on the other side. The moonlight glints off her face, showing all the lines that age brings. It's a strange sight after spending the past four years at court where no one looks over thirty.

"You don't have to knock, you can just walk in when you visit," I remind her.

She chuckles. "With newlyweds, it's always wise to."

A slight flush rises to my cheeks. She might not be wrong about that. "I'm sorry we didn't invite you to the wedding."

A strange smile crosses her face. "I'm grateful to have met my son's wife at all," she responds. "After he was taken from me for the last Golden Moon, I worried I'd never see him again. Having him so close by, and with you as his wife, is more than a mother could have asked for. I always hoped the two of you would last."

"I never realised," I say, a little overwhelmed by the admission from someone so important to Hector.

"The two of you were always close. I remember the day he told me that the two of you were courting. I'd been expecting it, but it made my heart glad. And now you're here."

"Not quite in the way any of us expected," I murmur.

"Perhaps not. But fate has a funny way of working. This is precisely where you're supposed to be, Agnes."

"It's where I want to be," I respond.

The door swings open and Hector steps inside with a basket of chicken eggs. "Mama, I didn't expect you tonight." He sets down the basket so he can hug her.

"I came to deliver a letter," she responds, holding it out to me. "It came from your brother."

"Thank you." I take it from her, trying not to feel too nervous about what Lincoln might have written. It's barely been a couple of days, I didn't think he'd be writing to us so soon.

"I'll leave you to it, but you should come for dinner once you're settled, I'll make your favourite." She reaches out to touch her son's cheek before making her way out of the door.

He starts unloading the chicken eggs.

"Did you get them yourself?" I ask.

"And face the terrifying chickens? Not a chance. One of the workers left them outside the coop for us."

"I hope they took some for themselves too," I respond.

"I believe so. What does Lincoln say?"

I lift the letter, turning it over in my hands. "I'm scared to open it," I admit. "He shouldn't be writing to us so soon, should he? What if he's telling us that we need to run?"

"I think if that was true, he'd have come himself," Hector assures me. "Open it. It probably won't be as bad as you think."

I take a deep breath. "All right." I run my fingers under the wax seal and pull out the sheet of paper. Lincoln's neat handwriting covers the page, and I read in silence, trying to make sense of exactly what he's saying.

I hand it to Hector once I'm done and he reads over it too. "Your father is angry."

"That's to be expected," I respond. "Lincoln said that he spent a whole day calling for both of our heads."

Hector puts an arm around me and pulls me close. "But it also says that Marcus talked him down and said that you should be banished and not allowed to return to court until your father gives you permission."

"I'm lucky to have the brothers I do." Fondness

for the two of them fills me, along with a little bit of worry that Father is going to take his anger out on the two of them.

I frown as I spot something on the back of the letter.

"What is it?" Hector asks.

"Something more." I take it back from him and turn it over, seeing a more hastily scribbled note. "It's a postscript saying that Father has decreed that we may return to court once we know which House you belong to and they claim you."

Hector raises an eyebrow. "I don't belong to any House."

"I suppose that's not true. You will be a noble's son, it's just that they didn't claim you at the Golden Moon ball." I turn the page over in my hands, trying to work out if there's more, but finding nothing.

"That's hardly going to change anything," he points out. "I'm just a royal guard."

"You're a prince consort," I counter. "That will change everything."

Though I'm not sure I like the idea of returning to court and playing the games of the noble Houses, but maybe it won't be so bad if I have Hector by my side.

Thank you for reading *Crown Of Blood And Duty*, I hope you enjoyed it! If you want to find out more about Linc, and see him break his vow to never marry, you can find him in *Rite Of Blood And Secrets*: https://books.authorlauragreenwood.co.uk/riteofbloodandsecrets

And if you want to read Agnes & Hector meeting for the first time in years from Hector's point of view, you can download it for free here: https://books.authorlauragreenwood.co.uk/hectorbonus

Author Note

Thank you for reading *Crown Of Blood And Duty*, I hope you enjoyed it!

There's lots to come in the *House Of Blood And Roses* series, with the main series following Beatrice as she attends the next Golden Moon Ball and discovers her true parentage in *Rite Of Blood And Secrets*. During the book, she also meets Lincoln - and as you might expect, he's definitely going to end up needing his sister's help!

I debated hard about what to write for this story. I wanted something that would be a strong taste of the series to come, while not giving away too many of the planned twists. In the end, there's just the one it gives away - that Lincoln is a Prince, but personally, I think the main series is going to be even more fun if you know that already! It's just Beatrice who has no idea who he is!

Agnes and Hector will be back later in the series, though for now they'll be living peacefully in their castle and staying far away from court politics!

If you want to keep up to date with new releases and other news, you can join my Facebook Reader Group or mailing list.

Stay safe & happy reading!

- Laura

Also by Laura Greenwood

You can find out more about each of my series on my website.

- Obscure Academy: a paranormal romance series set at a university-age academy for mixed supernaturals. Each book follows a different couple.
- The Apprentice Of Anubis: an urban fantasy series set in an alternative world where the Ancient Egyptian Empire never fell. It follows a new apprentice to the temple of Anubis as she learns about her new role.
- Forgotten Gods: a paranormal adventure romance series inspired by Egyptian mythology. Each book follows a different Ancient Egyptian goddess.
- Amethyst's Wand Shop Mysteries (with Arizona Tape): an urban fantasy murder mystery series following a witch who teams up with a detective to solve murders. Each book includes a different murder.
- Grimm Academy: a fantasy fairy tale academy series. Each book follows a different fairy tale heroine.

- Jinx Paranormal Dating Agency: a paranormal romance series based on worldwide mythology where paranormals and deities take part in events organised by the Jinx Dating Agency. Each book follows a different couple.
- Purple Oak Oasis (with Arizona Tape): a cozy fantasy romance series with unusual magic. Each book follows a different couple.
- House Of Blood And Roses: a vampire romantasy series following a heroine who discovers she's a vampire noble and has to navigate a world full of politics, betrayal, and blood lust.
- Scales Of Justice: an urban fantasy following a thief who accidentally becomes the newest apprentice of the goddess of truth.
- Speed Dating With The Denizens Of The Underworld (shared world): a paranormal romance shared world based on mythology from around the world. Each book follows a different couple.
- Blackthorn Academy For Supernaturals (shared world): a paranormal monster romance shared world based at Blackthorn Academy. Each book follows a different couple.

You can find a complete list of all my books on my website:

https://books.authorlauragreenwood.co.uk/book-list

Signed Paperback & Merchandise:

You can find signed paperbacks, hardcovers, and merchandise based on my series (including stickers, magnets, face masks, and more!) via my website:

https://books.authorlauragreenwood.co.uk/shop

About Laura Greenwood

Laura is a USA Today Bestselling Author of paranormal romance, urban fantasy, and fantasy romance. When she's not writing, she drinks a lot of tea, tries to resist French macarons, and works towards a diploma in Egyptology. She lives in the UK, where most of her books are set. Laura specialises in quick reads, with healthy relationships and consent-positive moments regardless of if she's writing light-hearted romance, mythology-heavy urban fantasy, or anything in between.

Follow Laura Greenwood

- Website: www.authorlaura-greenwood.co.uk
- Mailing List: https://books.authorlauragreenwood.co.uk/newsletter
- Facebook Group: http://facebook.com/groups/theparanormalcouncil
- Facebook Page: http://facebook.com/authorlauragreenwood

- Bookbub: https://www.bookbub.com/authors/laura-greenwood

Printed in Great Britain
by Amazon